Where's God?

Victor Kelleher

& Elise Hurst

Lothian
BOOKS

For the Peters of this world,
especially the ones who ask hard questions — V.K

For Mandy and Jane — E.H

Thomas C. Lothian Pty Ltd
132 Albert Road, South Melbourne, Victoria 3205
www.lothian.com.au

Text copyright © Victor Kelleher 2005
Illustrations copyright © Elise Hurst 2005

First published 2005

National Library of Australia
Cataloguing-in-Publication data:

Kelleher, Victor, 1939-

Where's God?
For children.

ISBN 0 7344 0748 3

1. God — Juvenile fiction. I. Hurst, Elise. II. Title.

A823.3

Designed by Georgie Wilson
Colour reproduction by Digital Imaging Group, Port Melbourne
Printed in China by SNP Leefung

'Where does God live?' Peter asked.

His big sister, Janet,
pointed to the ceiling.
'Up there.'

'D'you mean
in the attic?'

Janet went over to the window
and pointed at the sky.

'No. More kind of ... up there.'

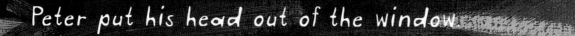

All he could see were clouds.

'I can't see anyone,' he said.

Janet coughed. 'God's not up there exactly.
He's more ...'

She coughed again.

'Listen. Why not ask Dad?'

Dad was reading the paper

'So where does God live?'
Peter asked him.
Dad waved a finger in the air.
'God? He's sort of ...
around.'

Around where?
wondered Peter.

He looked around the corner into the passage.

Nothing, except for an old skateboard.

He went and checked around the corner of the house.

Nothing, except for some bushes and his dog, Rocky.

Back inside, he said to Dad, 'I can't see God anywhere.'

Dad scratched his head and looked at Mum.
Mum said, 'It's like this. God's all over the place.

The screen door clanged and in walked Rocky.

'What about Rocky?' Peter asked. 'Is God in him too?'
Mum didn't seem very sure.

'Maybe. I mean ... it's possible.'

Peter narrowed his eyes so Rocky went fuzzy.
Then crossed his eyes so there were two Rockies.

But they both had the same doggy look.

'Would God really have a tail?' he asked.

Mum had had enough questions.

Peter could tell from the way her eyebrows scrunched together.

'I've told you,' she said. 'God's everywhere.
You've just got to learn how to look.'

Peter went outside to practise looking.

He saw a school bus go by.

Then a baby
in a pram.

Then
a kid on
a scooter.

They all
looked pretty
normal.

So did the postie who
stopped by the gate.

His face was red and sweaty like always.

'D'you know anything about God?' Peter asked him.

'Not a lot.
I mostly know about
where people live.
Addresses and stuff.'

'What's God's
address then?'

'Whew! That's
a hard one,'
the postie said.
'Why'd you ask?'

'I'm looking for Him.'

The postie pushed
back his hat and
thought for a while.

'Tell you what,'
he said at last.
'See the big church
on the corner?
That's where God's
supposed to live.
Try there.'

'Good idea,' said Peter, and set off.

There was
only one
other person
in the church.

A man in a
long black
robe. He was
standing
near a table
with a bright
gold cross
on it.

Peter walked over and
tugged at the man's robe.
'Is this your church?' he asked.
'It certainly is.'
'Then YOU must be God.'

The man seemed to think that was funny.

'No, I'm Father James,' he said. 'I just work for God.'

Peter pointed at the thick stone walls of the church. 'So all this belongs to God. It's really His house.'

'It's one of them,' Father James said. 'There are plenty of others. He owns houses like this all over the world.'

'Which one is He
living in right now?'
Peter asked.

'He's living in all of them
as far as I know.'

'All at the same time?'

'Yes,' Father James said
with a smile. 'It's a little
trick only God can do.'

'You mean a bit of Him's here
with us? At this very moment?'

'You could say that,'
Father James said.

Peter knelt down and looked under the nearest bench. He peered up at the roof. He lifted the altar cloth and searched there too.

'I can't see any bits,' he said.

Father James sighed. 'Aah, God can be difficult to find at times. Some people spend their whole lives looking for Him.'

'Do they find Him in the end?' Peter asked.

'Oh yes, they always find Him in the end.'

Peter thought about his Gramps. How old he was. And yet Gramps still hadn't reached the end. Dad said he had years and years left.

'The end sounds an awful long way off,' Peter said. 'I'd rather find God now.'

Father James
nodded sadly.
'I couldn't
agree more.'

'Well, I'd
better be
going,'
Peter said.
'There're
lots of other
places to
look.'

He left the church and walked on.

Further down
the street
Peter came to
Mrs Patel's
grocery store.

He liked Mrs Patel.
She was from
India. She had
a long plait and
a diamond stud
in her nose. Better
still, she told him
stories. About
elephants and lost
princesses and
dark jungles. She
also gave him
lollies when Mum
wasn't looking.

She gave him a
lolly now. As well
as a hug.

'What can I do
for you today?' she
asked. 'Have you
come for a story?'

Peter shook his head.
'No, I'm looking for
God today.'

'Which one?'

'You mean there's
more than one?'

Mrs Patel spread her
arms wide. 'Where I grew up
there are many gods.'

'Just one would do,'
Peter said.

'Then here is my favourite.'
Mrs Patel pointed to a
picture on the wall.
'This is the goddess Kali.
She watches over me.'

The woman in
the picture was very
beautiful. Also fierce
and scary.
Far too scary
for Peter's liking.

'Have you got any others?' he asked.

Mrs Patel pointed to a second picture.
Of a man with an elephant's head.

'This is Ganesh,'
she explained.
'He brings me good luck.'

Peter liked the look
of Ganesh. His long
trunk and flappy
ears reminded him
of Mrs Patel's
stories.

'Where does
this one live?'
he asked.

Mrs Patel pulled the same sad face as Father James.
'Who knows? In India perhaps. High in the mountains.'

Peter had never visited any mountains.
He didn't even know where India was.

'I need somewhere a bit closer,' he said.
'I think I'll look some more around here.'

Then he thanked Mrs Patel for the lolly and left.

Peter came to a small park at the end of the street. He saw an old man sitting on a bench. A ragged old man with a bristly chin and only one shoe.

Peter knew who he was. He had seen him at the shopping mall lots of times. People there called him Jim. They gave him money because he was poor.

Peter didn't have any money.
All he had was Mrs Patel's lolly.

He handed that
over instead.

Jim grinned. 'One good turn deserves another,
eh boy?' he said. 'So what can I do for you?'

'I'm looking for God,' Peter said. 'Any idea how
to find Him?'

'Easy,' Jim said. 'Me and God, we're best mates.'

'You know where He is then?'

'Sure I do. God's where He always is.' He pointed at Peter's chest. 'He's right in there.'

Inside me?'

'Where else? Go on, take a look.'

Peter closed his eyes and tried to look inside his head. It was so dark he couldn't see a thing.

'I can't see Him,' he said.

'That's because you're looking in the wrong place. God's in your heart, not your head.'

Then Jim popped the lolly into his mouth and also closed his eyes.

'You looking for God too?' Peter asked.

'No, I'm just enjoying the lolly,' Jim said.

Peter arrived home. Nothing much had changed.
Dad was still reading the paper. Mum and Janet
were watching TV.

'How do you look
inside your heart?'
Peter asked.

'Depends,' Mum
said.

'On what?'

'On what you're
looking for.'

'God.'

'Well your heart's
a good place
to start.'

'Yeah, but how
d'you get in there?'

Janet yawned.
'Haven't a clue.'

Dad rustled
his paper.
'Don't ask me.'

'Sorry, love,' Mum said. 'Can't really help you on that one.'

Peter went outside and sat on the back step.
Rocky came running over. He jumped up and
licked Peter's face.

Peter could
feel Rocky's
heart going

**boom
boom
boom**

Peter's own
heart answered   **boom
boom
boom**

Both hearts were making the same noise.

Maybe it was God talking to him. Maybe it wasn't.

Maybe he'd find out tomorrow.

Right now he'd had enough looking for one day.

He wanted to play with Rocky.